HYEWON KYUNG

BIGGER THAN YOU

GREENWILLOW BOOKS, *An Imprint of HarperCollinsPublishers*

www.harpercollinschildrens.com

The full-color art was created using hanji (traditional Korean
paper made from the mulberry tree), Korean paints,
and watercolors.
The text type is Futuramano Light.

Library of Congress Control Number: 2017956418
ISBN 978-0-06-268312-0 (hardcover)

18 19 20 21 22 SCP 10 9 8 7 6 5 4 3 2 1
First Edition

 Greenwillow Books

To Joy

Who wants to play with me?

I'm bigger than you.

I'm bigger than you.

I'm bigger than you.

I'm bigger than you.

I'm bigger than you.

I'm
bigger
than
you.

GRRRRRRRRRrr

I'm more **terrible** than you!

And I'm your mother!

Mom!

Now, are you all ready
to play together nicely?

Who wants to play with them on their prehistoric playground?

BIG	**BIGGER**	**MASSIVE**	**IMMENSE**
Dimetrodon	Minmi	Therizinosaurus	Iguanodon
How do you say it? **die-meh-TRUH-don**	How do you say it? **MIN-mee**	How do you say it? **there-uh-ZEEN-uh-SAWR-us**	How do you say it? **ig-WAN-oh-don**
Dimetrodon lived 280 million years ago.	Minmi lived 115 million years ago.	Therizinosaurus lived 70 million years ago.	Iguanodon lived 110–140 million years ago.

ENORMOUS
Triceratops

How do you say it?
try-SAIR-uh-tops

Triceratops lived
65 million years ago.

HUGE
Tyrannosaurus

How do you say it?
tuh-RAN-uh-SAWR-us

Tyrannosaurus lived
65 million years ago.

BIGGEST
Brachiosaurus

How do you say it?
BRACK-ee-uh-SAWR-us

Brachiosaurus lived
130–155 million years ago.

Simple machines are tools that make work easier
(and playing more fun).

A seesaw is a lever.

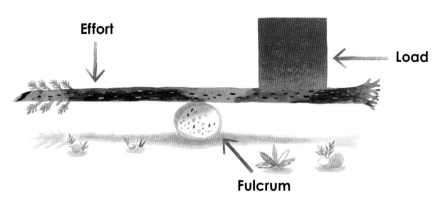

Effort

Load

Fulcrum

WHEE!

Grunt.

A slide is an inclined plane.

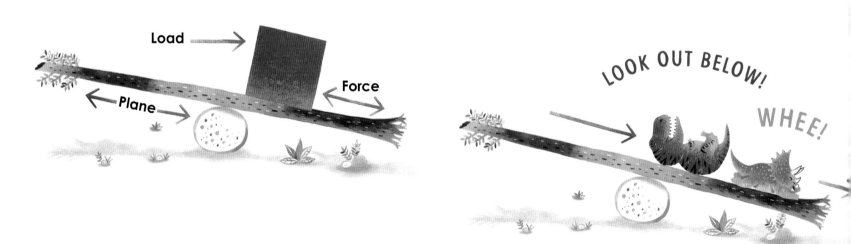

Load

Force

Plane

LOOK OUT BELOW!

WHEE!

There are simple machines all around you.
How many can you find? Try making your own simple
machines using sticks and rocks and blocks!